Reviews

'From start to finish, this is a book that is extremely difficult to put down! A beautiful, smart woman and the guy every woman dreams of are fighting not only against feelings forbidden according to ancient law, but for the lives of hundreds of people. You can almost touch the tension in this book. I cannot wait for the next installment from this author.'

Laura Clarke a Financial Advisor

'I'm not normally one for fiction, let alone fantasy so I picked up this book with a tiny bit of apprehension. A five star book for me is one that I have to tear myself away from and this has to be one of the better 5 star books I've read recently.

I could not put it down, regardless of whether I fit in the target demographic or not. I have no idea why I was so enamoured with this particular story but it just grabbed me, literally from the first chapter.

If you have an imagination and are willing to suspend your disbelief then you might enjoy this story. It's an extremely enjoyable read to while away a few hours but if your usual reading material tends to be the classics and nothing more, then this book is probably not for you.
Arousing in places, the story builds up nicely and the 'will they won't they' effect of Hayden and Amelia is engaging and fun. As a bit of a techie geek I enjoyed the GPS references. Her Vampire Guardian held my interest to the end - which many more literary books fail to do.'

Mark Mahabir a Senior IT Consultant

Reviews

The Art of Romance: Book 1
Her Vampire Guardian

Rebecca Wyatt

DragonEye Publishing

The Art of Romance: Book 1 – Her Vampire Guardian
Copyrighted © 2012 Rebecca Wyatt

First Edition
First Edition Printing October 2012

ISBN 13: 978-1-61500-023-4 (Paperback)
ISBN 13: 978-1-61500-082-1 (EPub ebook)
ISBN 13: 978-1-61500-184-2 (PDF)

Library of Congress Catalog Number: 2012942426

Published by Wolf's Moon, an Imprint of DragonEye Publishing

www.DragonEyePublishers.com
Orders@DragonEyePublishers.com

DragonEye Publishing
753 Linden Place, Unit A
Elmira, NY 14901 USA

Acknowledgements

Dedicated to those who I hold most dear, near or far you're forever in my thoughts. Thanks for being my motivation and my inspiration.

Introduction

Temptation is defined as a desire to do something wrong or unwise, desire; as a strong feeling of wanting.

For vampire guardian Hayden, Dr Amelia Jameson is the more accurate description. She's thrown the scientist stereotype out of the window! She's sexy, sassy and too tempting to be good, but when a break-in at her lab puts her in danger, it becomes evident there is nothing in this world - or the next - that Hayden won't do to protect her.

With passion and secrets building between them, can this unlikely couple resist each other? Or will they give into to their most primal needs and suffer the consequences?

The Art of Romance: Book1
Her Vampire Guardian

Chapter One

"How bad is the damage?"

Amelia Jameson did an inventory of her surroundings for the third time. Her eyes took in the devastation but she didn't see anything, her senses were engrossed in the soft, soothing voice emanating from the other end of her cell. It was like molten honey on a hot summer's day.

"Amelia! Are you hurt?!" How quickly that honey set to a hard, aggressive, urgent voice, demanding.

"I'm fine, but everything's destroyed." The lab had been trashed. Computers were smashed, tables were upturned and the floor was littered with paper. Hundreds of thousands of dollars worth of equipment lay scattered on the floor tiles in a million pieces. The walls of her laboratory were a standard clinical white, except for the window. It stretched from wall to wall and ceiling to floor, overlooking the city, but at 9 p.m., it was now dark outside. The night sky painted the glass black, creating a mirror that reflected the chaos. She stood there, staring at her reflection in the window. How did she end up here?

"I need to see for myself. Stay where you are, I'll be there in a few minutes." His voice was strained as he ended the call. What did he need to see for himself - the destruction, or that she was okay? She shook the idea out of her head before she let it take root. She was not going there.

Carefully, she made her way from one end of the lab to the other towards the vault, being careful not to disrupt any evidence. Glass crunched with each step as she neared the metal frame. There could be only one motive and as she placed her right index finger on the touch pad, she feared the worst. She held her breath and counted down the 8 seconds needed for fingerprint recognition. The panel flashed green three times before the door opened with a hiss. Empty.

"No, no, no!" She started to pace the room as she put a trembling palm to her forehead. Strong arms caught her as she turned, and pulled her into a solid body. The scents of coffee and vanilla filled her head, making her feel woozy. The aroma had unknowingly infiltrated her life over the past few months; normally she stayed away from caffeine but lately she'd found herself ordering a shot of vanilla in her latte. How pathetic.

His face was a distraction, so she saved that for last, knowing she wouldn't be able to form a coherent thought as soon as she caught a glimpse. For now, she savoured his embrace, let herself melt into him as she felt every line of his body against her and saw every plane through his tight dark shirt. Reluctantly, she stepped back and looked up severing physical contact but, oh, how he held her with his eyes. Beautiful, deep eyes, so rich they resembled chocolate and espresso. Her mouth started to water as she continued her usual inventory. His eyes were framed by long dark lashes that cast shadows upon his cheek, his jaw was dusted with dark stubble and his hair's texture was delicious - dark and glossy, and just long enough for her to run her fingers through and fist her hands in.

She shook the images out of her head; that could never happen, not for them. He wasn't just a vampire guardian, he was her guardian and there were rules against any kind of intimacy, it just complicated things. It occurred to her then that he always dressed in dark clothing, maybe it was a vampire thing. He was beautiful. He was midnight and equally as thrilling. She'd spent countless nights lusting after him. She had longed for him to turn up at her door and say that the law had been rewritten and that she could finally see those roped muscles she'd caught a glimpse of beneath his shirt. But it would never happen, could never happen, and the sooner she got over this stupid infatuation, the sooner she could find a real boyfriend. Someone to fulfill the fantasies she'd been building up over the last three months.

"What did you keep in here?" His voice broke through her thoughts and brought her back to the present.

"This isn't just a break-in, Hayden. Everything valuable has been broken - well, almost everything." She stepped away from the vault to emphasize her point. "My research and samples are missing".

'Sympathy for the Devil' by The Rolling Stones had become such a familiar tune since meeting Hayden and, instead of shouting, he calmly pulled his cell from his jacket and answered it.

Please allow me to introduce myself, I'm a man of wealth and taste... Yeah, she could definitely see the relevance in the song.

Now it was his turn to pace, talking too fast to for her to keep up; she had to walk over to the window to stop herself from reaching out to him. She just stood there, looking out into the city as raindrops beat against the glass. Someone, somewhere down there, had the power to bring chaos and destruction to Minnesota and it would be all her fault.

A few minutes later, Hayden's reflection appeared behind hers. The contrast between them was staggering. He was everything she wasn't, and the realization made her sick to her stomach.

"That was Elijah. There's good news and there's bad news." She leaned forward, pressed her forehead against the cool glass and closed her eyes. If she felt nauseous before, it was nothing compared to the dread churning in her gut. She inhaled deeply then let it go in one quick exhalation. A hundred things ran through her mind. Elijah was head of the vampire clan in Minnesota - did he see her as a liability to their cause? Were they cutting her loose, no longer willing to protect anyone who couldn't even protect her own research? How could she have been so stupid?!

"What's the bad news?" Best to get it over with, she thought. He rested a firm hand on her shoulder, silently giving her support, he'd never know how much that meant to her.

"The break-in is a complication, but one he hadn't ruled out. He's got Jackson speaking to contacts to see if he can find out anything useful."

From what Hayden had told her, the clan was split into three ranks: Guardian, Defender and Warrior. In short, Defenders were all about the tactics. They were the brains of the operation, deciding when, where, who and how to go about a situation. Warriors were front line. They were sent in to get the job done and Guardians, well, in her opinion, they were just glorified babysitters.

"And the good news?"

"Until this mess is sorted we're going to hang out. You're not leaving my side, Em."

"That's good news?" Until she'd met Hayden, her father was the only one who called her Em. Hearing it from Hayden made her heart race every time the word left his lips. It was personal, endearing and reminded her of her father in a way that wasn't too painful to remember.

"I think so. At least I'll finally get to find out what you do with your Friday evenings." He did that brooding thing with his eyes, as if he was stripping away the walls around her soul before changing the direction of the conversation. "Clean up will be here soon, there's no need for us to stick around. You look like you could use a hot shower. I'll drive you home."

It was a Friday like any other. He'd picked her up from her apartment this morning and driven her to work, all the time imagining the conversation they would have if he asked to accompany her again this evening. They'd had this conversation near enough every day since they'd met, and still he didn't tire of it. If he was being honest, he loved the fire in her eyes and the tone she used when she turned him down. That was the only condition she insisted upon when she agreed to the protection detail - that Friday evenings were her own. He could drop her off at home every day and stay all night if necessary, except for Fridays. At the time it was easy enough to agree to but as each week passed it became a challenge, another piece to the Amelia puzzle he wanted to know.

Now a whirlpool of emotions flooded his system, crashing like tidal waves. He couldn't control his anger at whoever had trashed the lab, and his anger at himself. He was supposed to be keeping watch over her and this was the second time in as many months she'd been close to being hurt. The first was little over a week into the protection detail. He'd given her a little space when she went on a date - even then he'd hated the thought of someone else gazing at her from across a table, brushing their fingers against hers and trying for a goodnight kiss at the end of the evening. He'd followed the pair from bar to bar, staying in the shadows. Amelia wasn't the sort of girl who'd offer herself so quickly, so when the jerk had walked her home and then tried to push his way into her apartment, he had taken great satisfaction in unleashing a world of pain on the guy. Last thing he heard he was just about breathing on his own now. Pity.

Something dark had unfurled inside him that night. Sure, he was her guardian, but this was something more. Instinctively he knew that if harm ever came to Amelia he'd be hurting too - the only way that that should be possible would be if they were mated. Two souls becoming one; but they hadn't mated, and they couldn't. There was too much at stake for him, yet still, the thought of her finding happiness with another man made him want to grab her by the waist and challenge any man, vampire or beast who thought they could take her from him. Ultimately he knew he'd have to let her go. He'd always be her guardian, her protector, but they could never be anything more; the sooner he dealt with that the easier his life would be.

He looked every inch of her over while he waited for her to put the CCTV tape into her bag and grab some papers. He told himself it was just to ensure she wasn't harmed - that was his job after all. Although he was a vampire, he was also her guardian and it was his responsibility to make sure she was safe at all times. She'd called him a couple of hours ago to let him know she was heading into a last minute meeting; he hadn't liked it. She gave him a copy of her daily schedule so he always knew where she was; last minute things had him on edge. Now he was eternally grateful for it. If she'd arrived back at her lab ten minutes earlier, she'd have been in the thick of the raid. She would have been hurt, if not captured and killed. The thought alone made a red mist cloud his vision and he felt anger start to throb in his veins.

"Okay, I need to hand this tape in at reception for when the Police arrive. It's probably best we're not here when that happens - let's go."

Big, emerald-green eyes had him drowning, with no hope of rescue. Every ounce of tension in his body seemed to seep out of his pores and disappear, just by looking into those eyes. Her cheekbones were high and defined and currently flushed a pretty shade of pink, but those lips - they were the real prize. Full, pink, begging to be taken. He could barely contain his groan as he watched them part and her tongue sweep out and over them leaving them plump and moist as if she'd read his thoughts.

He walked her across the parking lot to his car, checking every shadow. The night air helped him to put things into perspective. She was safe now that she was with him, so he could relax a little and enjoy whatever the evening would bring.

The drive to her apartment from the lab only took fifteen minutes, but the silence made it seem longer. There were stories about vampires being able to read minds, but that wasn't the case; he'd often wondered what she really thought of him. Was he a monster she'd been paired with, or did she desire him also? He wouldn't be able to handle either response, so not knowing seemed to be the only answer.

The rain came down in fat wet drops soaking them both through to the skin as they ran from the car to her building.

She thought back to that day she was approached by Elijah, her paper on the effects of blood types on parasites had just been published. He seemed like any other investor, asking about her methods - endless questioning. After a few days, he turned up at her lab and explained the reasons his kind were interested in her work, as well as the positive and negative effects it could have on both their species and her own, should her research fall into the wrong hands. She'd listened and looked at the proposal rationally, before reluctantly agreeing to a babysitter. It was then 3 months, 18 days, 9 hours and around 28 minutes ago that Hayden had turned up at her door.

She was a doctor of Hematology. She'd graduated with honors from the University of Minnesota Medical School, and had dedicated her time to studying the prevention of blood diseases, ever since her father died of a rare blood disease 6 years ago; all things considered, it kind of made sense that vampires would be interested in her work. According to Hayden, she'd become a temporary member of the clan and as long as her work benefited them, she would be protected by him. Her own personal guardian - there to ensure no harm came to her, by anyone or anything.

Since then, her budget had tripled and rather than looking at ticks under a microscope, her guinea pigs were vampires from the clan who volunteered themselves to assist in her research. Her one-bed apartment was now a suite, and rather than hail a cab to and from the lab each day, Hayden now drove her anywhere she needed to go. Except on Friday evenings - but that would soon all change.

Tonight wasn't like any other. Hayden usually dropped her off home and left every evening, but never wandered too far; occasionally he'd come inside for a drink and position himself in her favorite overstuffed armchair. She loved having him close by, but looking at him standing in her living room tonight filled her with irritation. Tonight was supposed to be her escape from everything. The clan, the ones they protected her from, and almost everything else. She didn't want her piece of salvation tainted by today, and she wasn't ready to share it with anyone yet, was she?

"Erm, considering everything that's happened I'm not entirely sure going out tonight is such a great idea. I'll probably just grab takeout, open a bottle of wine and stay here. You're welcome to join me," she fought to make her tone indifferent, but he didn't look convinced. God, how she wanted him to stay with her tonight. She wanted him every night, so whenever he finished an inventory of the apartment and wished her a good night before leaving, a small piece of her died.

His smile was full of mischief, like a child who knew they'd eventually get their own way - so, so sexy. It made her mouth go dry.

"I'm disappointed you think I'd let you off the hook like that. Every Friday night for the past three months you've got me to drop you off at home, then leave. The one time I made you late and offered to drive you to wherever it is you go, you threatened to stake me." Her breath caught as he cautiously lifted his hand and brushed away a strand of hair that had escaped her ponytail. "If I wasn't sure you'd go through with it then I'd have followed you, but whatever it is, it seems to mean a lot to you." Surely he was more myth than man; dark, mysterious and incredible looking, with a heart that called out to hers. "So," Hayden continued, unaware of her internal dilemma, "I'm not going to let some jackass vampire ruin my opportunity to find out where you sneak off to! Unless you want to go dressed like that, I suggest you change."

She let out an exasperated sigh and met his eager gaze - clearly he wasn't about to give up. She stood, crossed her arms over her chest and leveled him with an intense gaze before walking over to stand over him. The power play excited her. "Fine, but if you're coming with me, then you have to agree to a few things. Firstly, you have to keep your mouth shut - on the way there, when we get there and most definitely when we leave. Secondly, what happens tonight stays between you and I. If you utter a word of this to anyone I will stake you."

He stood fluidly, his lips ended up barely an inch from hers. He'd taken control again, and she loved it. She gasped as he bent forward half an inch, he was so close. If she stuck her tongue out she could trace the outline of his lips; her cheeks blushed in anticipation and her heart pounded so loud and hard, she thought it would rip free of her chest. He raised his cycbrows at the close proximity - his lips parted but never touched hers as he spoke softly, "The only promise I'll make you tonight is the same promise I make you every night. No matter what happens, I'll keep you safe."

His eyes held hers for what seemed like an eternity before they dropped to her mouth. He gently ran a slender finger from her temple down to her jaw, and then across her lower lip.

"I've wondered how these lips would feel, how they would taste. I long to find out, but I can't. Every moment I spend with you, unable to touch you, is torture."

"I - I'm sorry…" she didn't know what else to say, so turned her face away from the intensity of his gaze. She was scared that she would stop fighting and give into the most delicious temptation, but he caught her face in his hands before she could.

"Don't ever be sorry. I fear that not being with you would be a far worse hell".

He left her alone while she showered, although his eyes lingered on the bathroom door after he watched her disappear inside. Listening to her switch on the water, he thought of her standing there naked under the torrent. He contemplated how good it would have felt after her traumatic day.

Imagining her bracing herself against the fogged glass, and rubbing soapy hands over her soft flesh, he wanted to watch as the water ran down her breasts and over her beautifully toned torso, then down her incredibly long legs, washing away the lather to reveal her ivory soft skin underneath. He wanted to taste her. Mark her. Claim her.

His body reacted to the thoughts and ached to join her, pushing her up against the wet tiles and lifting her hips so she could wrap those legs around his waist, he wanted to bury himself inside her and forget everyone and everything but her. Fuck! He reached inside his jeans to adjust himself - he'd never been this hung up over a woman before; sure, he'd had lovers in the past, but all of those women combined didn't hold a tenth of the attraction that he felt towards Amelia. Of course in being her guardian, they'd form a bond, but this was different, this was something more.

He couldn't deny that Amelia made him feel things - some were to be expected, like sexual arousal. She was beautiful and he was only … a man. But there were feelings that were foreign to him, like this pull in his chest he felt whenever she wasn't around, but above all, curiosity. Humans were normally so predictable but this little human - his Amelia - constantly had him guessing. Everything about her had him curious: the tattoo he'd seen through a white shirt when it rained, why she wore sexy heels with her lab coat and where the hell she disappeared to every Friday evening.

He knew not to get too involved, a guardian couldn't become intimate with whomever he was protecting, it made for an over-protective bond that put the people around them at risk. It'd happened only once before; Duggan had lashed out at everyone who came into contact with Giselle until eventually the council assigned her a new guardian and banished Duggan, but the bond had worked both ways and soon living without him proved too much for Giselle. A few weeks later she gave up everything - her job, her family and anything that had ever mattered to her. She'd tracked down her lover and the pair were now living in exile, not needing anyone or anything other than each other.

To feel that way about someone was ridiculous, but sort of beautiful, and although time and time again he'd denied himself a female, the thought of Amelia making that kind of sacrifice for him made his chest puff up in pride.

He tried to rein himself back in to the present but his thoughts were totally dominated by Amelia; his strange attraction to her was probably superficial, a product of the fact that she was the first young female he'd been assigned to. You'd have to be blind not to realize how beautiful she was, but the facts remained the same. He was a vampire, her guardian sent to protect her, as long as she was of some use to the clan and its cause.

She was a mere mortal, capable of cruel actions, harsh words and dying.

No. Tonight was about keeping an eye on her, and satisfying only his curiosity. A quick glance at his watch showed she'd been in there for twenty minutes, she'd be finishing her shower soon, but there was still enough to time for a quick call to Jackson, head of the Defenders, to get an update. The phone only rang once before a gruff voice answered: "I take it you're calling for the latest?" Hayden admired him, the guy was definitely the man for the job.

"Have you got anything new for me?"

"We picked up a couple of rogues a few hours ago, fangs for hire, it would seem. Information was very sketchy but it sounds like it's Seccombe pulling the strings. He has the research but it doesn't look like he's figured out what it means yet."

"She was instructed to encode all of her work in case something like this should happen. That should buy you enough time to find it before he realizes what he has."

"There's something else, there was mention of a list amongst the things taken."

"What kind of list?"

"Names. I don't know anything more than that. Perhaps the good doctor could shed some light on the matter?"

"I'll talk to her."

"Make sure you do, you have 24 hours." With that, he ended the call.

The shower had slowed her pulse and calmed her for the time being, but the thought of Hayden's lips against hers sent a shock to her long dormant heart. She couldn't let herself begin to hope. As she stepped out of the shower stall, she realized belatedly that all of her clothes were in the bedroom. She'd been so desperate to escape the intensity of his gaze, she'd almost run to the shower. Now, left with no option other than nudity, she grabbed the soft white bathrobe that hung on the back of the bathroom door. Feeling a little self-conscious about being completely naked underneath it, she tightened the belt and stepped out of the bathroom.

She found Hayden in the bedroom. Leaning up against the doorjamb, she watched as he moved around the room, silently opening drawers and looking inside, scanning the books on the shelves and running his fingers over everything in reach. She was able to pinpoint the second he sensed her by the way in which the muscles in his shoulders tensed. Slowly, he turned and took in the sight of her. She knew what he saw; her skin was ivory, with long damp hair that trailed down her back. Even in this light she was able to make out the widening of his eyes, before he swiftly retreated to the window, putting up walls and distance between them.

She cleared her throat. "I just need a little more time to finish getting ready, help yourself to a drink. I think there's a beer in the fridge or a bottle of scotch on the table in the living room, but I guess you shouldn't drink if you're going to drive, but then I don't know if alcohol affects you like it effects humans … and I'm rambling again."

"I like it when you ramble, there's an innocent truth in the things you say."

"So - are you going to get a drink?" that was any normal man's cue to leave, but he just stood there at the opposite side of the room allowing his gaze to travel the length of her body.

"No, I'm not."

He showed no sign of leaving, did he actually expect her to change while he stood there staring? A display of power, perhaps. Well, fine - if he thought she would balk at his little power play, he was wrong.

All her life, she'd stuck to the rules; one of her most important ones involved buying an outfit to match her shoes, rather than the other way round. Her Christian Louboutin peep toes were calling out to her. Just looking at their beauty and blood-red soles cheered her up considerably. They were all she'd wanted for ages and now that she had a few dollars to spare she was finally able to indulge.

Tonight was their maiden voyage, so she needed an outfit that would do them justice. She walked over to her closet and pulled out her favorite dresses and sprawled them across her bed. Blood-red chiffon that came to her calves accentuating her breasts - she wanted to capture attention but perhaps the red dress and red soles were overkill. Next, a long black number - very conservative, but perhaps a little boring. Finally, her favorite - although she hadn't worn it in years - a knee-length backless dress in electric blue silk. It was elegant and sophisticated, with a plunging neckline and spaghetti straps. With the help of her shoes, it really ramped up the 'sexy'.

Decision made, she turned to face Hayden, the rise and fall of his chest was rapid, equaled by the tremors she felt as their eyes met. His gaze held hers as she slowly unfastened the belt and let it fall open; his breathing hitched but his eyes never left hers so she let the fabric fall and pool around her ankles, pushed her shoulders back and silently counted to three. When she opened her eyes he was gone.

Her lips twitched at the corners. "Not so brave, huh, vampire?" she muttered as she continued to dress. Soon enough she was ready to leave, with her hair styled so the loose curls fell against the flesh of her back - it was raining outside so it would only curl when it got wet anyway. She checked her lipstick again and once satisfied, she left the bedroom and walked into the living room, where she knew Hayden would be waiting. His words weren't coherent as she walked past him to grab her coat, but she took that as a "Yeah, you look nice."

She's always wondered why he drove a car at all. The guy could phase anywhere - literally disappear and transport his physical body anywhere in seconds. She hadn't asked about it for fear of sounding like an utter idiot, but she couldn't relax against the black leather seats of his Mercedes like she usually could. They were currently eight minutes into an awkward silence that had her on edge.

"Why do you drive?"

The question clearly caught him off guard but he answered anyway: "What you mean is, why do I drive when I can phase from place to place?"

"I guess..." she dropped her eyes to her Loubies and the blue nail polish on her toes.

"Sometimes driving helps you to appear normal when you park your car and walk into a shop, rather than just appearing there."

"I suppose that makes sense."

"And sometimes it's a necessity. I'm not sure how you'd react to being here one minute, then Barcelona the next".

"Wow, I always thought of you going from my place to yours, I can't even comprehend international trips." The silence was back, heavier than before. "So - can you phase with someone then?"

"I can but it drains every ounce of energy I have and makes me sick."

"Sounds like you've been through it before?"

"Something like that."

She knew there was something more - something he kept from her - but she had her own secrets, so could allow him his.

"What did you find out about the break-in at my lab?"

"Aren't you full of questions tonight? What makes you think I've heard anything more?" His voice was far huskier than usual; she figured it was either because he was actually mad at her about the break-in, or because he didn't know what to say after her little striptease earlier. Tension rolled off him in waves, but that only seemed to make him sexier.

"I figured that's where you phased to … earlier." Her voice broke on the last word when she saw his knuckles turn white as his grip on the steering wheel tightened.

"Seccombe has your research."

That shut her up. The vampire was bad news as far as she knew and any kind of interest he had in her work was not good. Elijah had warned her what could happen if her research fell into the wrong hands. A cold shiver chased up her spine and started to take residence in her heart. This was her fault and sitting here next to the one man who would die for her if necessary, she made a silent vow: she'd do anything - anything at all - to save him and those she'd almost certainly sentenced to death.

They pulled up against the curb outside Indigo; the rain had picked up so considerably that as she looked up at the pulsing club sign, she could have sworn the car was submerged in water. She exited the car as the valet approached with an umbrella and a lustful grin, which quickly vanished at the sound of Hayden's car door closing.

Entry into the club wasn't a problem, she was a regular with a recognizable face, and as she dodged a queue of people promising unspeakable things in exchange for entry, the doorman allowed her in with a smile. "Miss Amelia, so good to see you again, are you working tonight?"

"You know, I don't think of it as work, Jake." The doorman was in his early twenties with grey eyes and light hair - cute, but not her type.

"I'll see you inside later then."

"I doubt that very much." The harsh words came from her chaperone, his face was a blank mask but his eyes promised pain.

She stepped through the doorway with Hayden close at her heels. If she was honest with herself, she'd spent far too much time looking at that face recently, reading too much into his every word and expression.

As always, she took the descent down the stairs slowly - not because the staircase was dark with only a row of tiny lights running along the edge of each step, but because she loved the dark, felt safe in it; it heightened her senses and helped her lose herself in the atmosphere. Her hand reached out, but not to grope the banister. She ran her fingertips over the velvet-embossed wall covering, and although physically and emotionally exhausted from the break-in at her lab, she could feel her spirits lifting as she entered the vast room that stretched out before her. The floor was a sea of dark, deep plush carpet so luxurious she was usually guilty of shedding her shoes and walking around barefoot. The walls were covered in the same exquisite paper and thick velvet drapes, and the lighting reflected off every shiny surface, bathing the inhabitants in a bruise-like purple. Indigo.

She knew the second Hayden left her to check out the perimeter, because the warmth she'd grown used to over the last few hours was suddenly gone. She couldn't become dependent on him. She was nothing more than just another job to him - a name and an obligation. Well, that was fine, she'd pay him no more attention than courtesy absolutely demanded. To one side of the room, a cavernous dance floor dominated the space next to the stage, where a young man in his twenties was setting up a microphone and guitar; on the other side a contemporary bar stretched the length of the room and was surrounded by seating. The club was exclusive and always brimming with humans and super naturals. She'd sung here herself in the past but the more time her work demanded, the less time she had for her real passion.

Thinking about work again had her pulse racing as dread filled her stomach. When she'd called the Police to report the break-in, they'd questioned her, asking if she knew anyone who could be responsible. She'd given the name of her assistant she'd fired just before Hayden had made an appearance in her life. She had caught him trying to sell her research to another corporation and, although she knew he wasn't responsible tonight, the guy was no doubt guilty of other crimes. Why not point them in his direction and let them do a little digging?! The one truly responsible would never be punished by law enforcement - well, not the sort that involved handcuffs and prison cells. No - when the clan tracked him down, there would be a fight to the death and Seccombe would lose. He had to. She tried to divert the ever-growing dark thoughts running through her mind, so with a deep inhalation she made her way over to the bar.

Dan had worked as a barman here for as many years as she'd been coming, so nowadays he all but reserved her a seat. He was handsome and easy to be with, so she'd accepted his offer of dinner not long after they'd met but after a few dates and an awkward kiss, they'd both realized they wouldn't be anything other than friends. It had been Dan who encouraged her to sing at the club and she loved him for that. As soon as he caught sight of her, his eyes lit up as he gestured towards a stool, and when she was seatcd hc poured a glass of champagne then leaned over the bar to kiss her cheek as he asked about her day.

"It's been hell, I can't tell you how much I need this." Drinking swiftly, she finished and passed the flute back for a refill.

"In that case, this is on me." He topped up her glass, before moving on to serve his other customers. She sipped at the golden liquid as her eyes swept the room, doing a casual check on the club's occupants - God, she was turning into Hayden!

Her eyes fell upon a man standing against the dark drapes in the corner of the room. He didn't have a drink or a date; instead, he just stood there, his eyes locked with hers. Was he scowling? It was impossible to tell from here, but no measure of distance could mask the fact that he really was something to look at, dressed in jeans and boots. She took in the sight of him - the dark shirt he wore almost enabled him to blend into the background, his only giveaway was the honey-blonde hair tied at his nape. Only the movement of him approaching cleared the fog that had descended on her brain and made her eyelids heavy, she gave herself a mental slap for not realizing sooner that he wasn't human.

Her breath quickened with every step he took, but before he could reach her, his path was blocked. Hayden towered over him like an avenging angel. She pushed her stool out and went to stand close by, eager to hear the interaction between the two men, but before she even formulated then plan in her head Hayden held a hand up to her, a gesture to stop. He hadn't even looked in her direction; he just knew what she would do and had stopped her.

Chapter Two

Hayden had given both floors of the club and the storage rooms a once-over before he had returned to the bar area; he needed a few minutes away from her to let his aggression simmer, instead of boiling over. Almost every guy here wanted to make a play at her, including someone of the humans who were already taken. And then there'd been the barman's gaze - his eyes had dipped to Amelia's chest almost as frequently as he'd touched her unnecessarily. Every time he'd stroked her arm or pushed her hair behind her ear, Hayden's hands balled up to fists at his sides. Why was he so fucking jealous? Since when had he felt this level of protectiveness over anyone? And why the hell did he want to punch that guy for not allowing those dark curls to tumble free around her face?

He'd watched as Amelia downed her first drink then turned her back on him before scouting the room. She wouldn't know, but that was her natural instincts detecting danger, and that danger currently came in the form of Travis McCroy, a rogue vampire. Their paths had crossed once or twice in the past. Hayden had been monitoring the vampire from the shadows; he had his eyes fixed on Amelia in a way he wouldn't tolerate and as soon as he'd taken a step towards her the guardian had intervened. He opened his mouth to demand the blonde vampire's intentions, but before he had the chance his unspoken question was answered.

"Will you surrender the doctor and renounce your protection over her?" His voice was as deadpan as his eyes, and that wasn't a good thing.

"Never." Although only a single word, it held enough authority and truth as if he'd spoken a million.

"And if she chooses it?"

"She won't." Hayden was certain of that. Not because he meant anything to her, but because she cared about the greater good and knew what could happen if Seccombe gained more power.

"You're foolish, guardian. A change in the hierarchy is inevitable and when it comes around, I think I'll take great pleasure in your little human. If you're lucky, I might let you live long enough to watch."

Pure rage pounded through his veins and that red mist descended over his vision again; this creature even thought to lay a hand on his woman! Before he could unleash a world of pain on the blonde vampire, it phased. Of course, he could follow the energy trail left behind by any supernatural but that would leave Amelia vulnerable, so he rubbed his hand down his face and turned to head to the bar. He caught the barman's attention and demanded two fingers of scotch, before drinking it back as Amelia had.

"What happened with the creep from the crypt?" Her voice was almost lost as the crowd started to sing along to the live acoustics on stage.

"Nothing you need to worry about. What are we here for anyway?" he wished he didn't sound like such a jerk but what else was he supposed to say? He ordered another two fingers and reveled in the look of fear on the barman's face, before he turned to Amelia.

"Hey honey, you're up." The guy took one more look at him before scurrying off to the far end of the bar, suddenly busy. Smart move.

"You sing?" the surprise in his tone gave him away. She gave a hint of a smile before answering, "Kind of."

He watched as she drained the remaining golden liquid in her glass, and headed up the steps to the stage. She claimed the stool at the piano, put her fingers to the keys and started to play. Never before had he heard such an enchanting sound; he didn't recognize the song but he still adored it. She tamed the elegant beast, and when he finally was able to force his eyes away from the magic emanating from her slender fingertips he looked up to her face. Eyes closed, she rocked back and forth as if it would make the music sweeter. Each note was perfect and flowed effortlessly into the next, she had the voice of an angel, and as he looked around the now silent crowd, the emotion was clear to see. There were people crying with joy and others holding onto their loved ones. He could do neither, he wasn't capable of tears and the one person he cared about was up on that stage bewitching him.

After an immeasurable amount of time the music stopped and applause filled the room, and then she was there, standing next to him again. His Amelia - the scientist, musician and the sexiest little human in existence.

"That was good, really good"

She gave him a coy smile that told him she was reluctant to discuss her talent, so he cleared his throat and got back to business.

"His name is Travis, he's working for Seccombe."

"Where did he go?"

"I don't know where, or how long for." He didn't want to taint this moment, to talk about work after such a beautiful performance was criminal, but inevitable.

"I need to take you someplace you're going to be safe. I want you to come home with me." He let the words hang there - unsure of her response.

"I'm tired of being afraid, Hayden. I don't want to waste my life running away."

"Then come with me so you don't have to!" She seemed to consider his offer for a moment, before giving a slight nod of agreement and that's all it took to undo him. He stepped into her, wedging her between the bar and his body, ready to claim her mouth with a primal need he'd never experienced before. He felt every soft curve of her body against his - nothing had ever felt this good. Just a breath away from those pretty pink lips and the heat they promised, he closed his eyes and deeply inhaled her scent. It was sweet, sweet torture, but he managed to maintain control of himself; if he gave into lust now he'd have her up against the bar.

His eyes raked over her body. He'd never been so hungry. Her hair was a dark halo, tumbling down her back in loose curls in such a contrast to her pale skin that made him think of strawberries and cream. The urge to see if she tasted just as sweet was overwhelming but it was too public here. When he had her – and he would have her – it would just be the two of them, her beneath him with her nails in his back. The thought made him strain against his zipper to the point of pain.

She tried to hide the blush in her cheeks as the length of him, restricted by denim, pressed against her stomach; she straightened her dress and asked him if he wanted another drink before leaving.

Yes I want a drink. I want to drink you and feel your blood caressing my heart as it's pumped through my veins. I want to make you scream my name as I devour every inch of you.

He cleared his throat and his head, now was not the time for those kinds of thoughts, he had to remain focused but it was almost impossible with such temptation within reach.

"No, we really need to get going. We'll stop by your place on the way so you can pick up some clothes," his voice was hushed, he knew only too well how sensitive the hearing of super naturals was, and he didn't want to attract any more unwanted attention. Already a group of nomads was eyeing her up as if she was an appetizer; he was severely outnumbered.

"How long will I be staying with you for?" She wasn't able to mask the hesitation in her voice and he found himself soothing her by making small circles into the back of her hand, with his thumb marveling at the texture and heat of her skin as they reached the exit.

"However long it takes."

The trip from her apartment to his place in Minneapolis was quick, which was both good and bad. It gave her just enough time to collect the bare essentials from her apartment and consider her current situation without freaking out, but on the downside, she was literally walking into her own personal living hell. The mental walls she'd built to keep everyone out were slowly starting to crumble and there was nothing she could do about it.

"I want you to stay in my room." Her heart seemed to beat a hundred times a second.

"Why?"

"Don't question me, woman! Just, please, do as I ask!" He led the way straight through the house, not bothering with a guided tour, and stopped only when he reached what she imagined was the master bedroom. The door opened up to reveal an exquisite room decorated in dark blue drapes, antique furniture and a huge four-poster bed covered with light sheets and a comforter that matched the curtains. The wooden floor was dark and creaked as Hayden crossed the room to open the door to an adjoining bathroom the size of her entire apartment.

"There are fresh towels in the cupboard - help yourself to anything else you need," Hayden announced as he walked over to the antique loveseat under the window and put her suitcase down before sitting there himself.

"Where will you sleep?"

"I won't be sleeping much, but I thought I'd stay here," he tapped his palms on the fabric, "So I'm close by, in case you need me."

Her mouth went dry and she found it hard to talk. "I thought you said it was safe here…" The look he gave her was a brooding one and told her that there was nowhere else in the world she'd be safer.

"It's been a long day; you should try to get some sleep."

He left her alone while she showered, muttered something about needing to check protection wards were still in place, but the look on his face told her that it was more likely he couldn't cope with a replay of her shower this morning. She groped the tiled wall until she found the light switch, the room was covered in floor-to-ceiling white tiles, except for the huge blue mosaic in the centre of the room, of which she recognized the symbol as the clan's crest. There were fresh towels as promised and a full-length mirror opposite the shower; it wasn't long before her thoughts drifted to images of Hayden's reflection as he showered. He would be so beautiful she'd beg to kiss every inch of his skin, to lick the rivulets of water that would run the length of his abdomen and pool in his navel, and his tattoo. He'd told her about it but she hadn't seen it yet. He had a dragon that covered his entire left shoulder, and how she wanted to see it, caress it and watch as hot water beaded across the surface.

She showered quickly but efficiently, and moved back to the bedroom, securely tucked up in a huge white towel. She was pleased that Hayden wasn't back in the room yet, it gave her time to take in every corner and crevice. Every artifact within the room caught her attention and made her wonder about the story behind it. After snooping for a few minutes, she opened the closet and pulled out one of the shirts to sleep in.

There was a gentle rapping at the door, followed by the most heavenly and innocent voice: "Em, Can I come in?"

She made her way over to the ornate door and inhaled deeply the scent of him that still clung to the fabric - more vanilla than coffee - and when she eventually opened the door his gaze became feral, as his eyes dropped to her borrowed clothing.

"I - I'm sorry. I didn't bring anything to sleep in and you said to help myself to anything I needed so -"

"No, it's fine."

"Are you sure? I can change…"

"Honestly, it's okay. I'm just not used to having people about the house, let alone half-naked women!"

The shirt looked older than the rest - that's why she'd picked it. Pinching the fabric around the chest area, she asked, "Is this your favorite shirt?"

A wry smile threatened to cross his lips as he walked past her and made his way over to the loveseat. She figured that he wasn't going to reply, so she too crossed the room and climbed into bed. It was soft and inviting but absolutely huge - hardly surprising, considering the size of its usual occupant. The cold sheets felt good against her warm over-sensitized skin, and she soon found herself curling up on her side and inhaling the scent of Hayden that clung to the pillows.

"It is now," and, with that, Hayden was the last thought she had as she drifted off to sleep.

When she awoke, the sun was high in the sky and the stiffness in her limbs told her that she'd been sleeping for a long time; there was no confusion about where she was, although she felt a pang of regret that she couldn't see him first thing in the morning, hair mussed and sleepy-eyed.

Her dreams had been haunted by the vampire at the club. "Oh, I have such plans for you," he'd said, followed by visions of her chained to a bed while he sank his teeth into flesh. "Renounce your protection, come to me and I shan't harm any other." Even after she'd woken up she couldn't shake the images from her head.

The sound of clattering pans and cursing caused her to venture out of the bedroom and head down the hall in search of Hayden. She hadn't noticed last night how big everything was, for it had been a dark night with no moon and, because of the rain, she'd run from the car to the house without looking at the sheer magnitude of it. She hadn't been able to look around the house because he had taken her straight to his room, but now she was able to peek into each room and bask in the pure luxury of Hayden's estate. The view from the window showed acres of land, dotted with large trees, high iron fencing and an electric gate. She guessed the babysitting business paid well.

Soon, she found herself distracted by heavenly smells emanating from what she imagined was the kitchen. When she entered the bright room she was shocked to find him at the stove.

"Talk about sleeping like the dead!" he called over his shoulder. Did she detect a hint of humor in his tone? Great, a guy that laughed at his own jokes.

"Yeah, I guess I kind of slept most of the day. You should've woken me." She still stood in the doorway as he turned to look at her; as soon as he laid his eyes on her, he dropped the frying pan and gripped the counter for support.

"Holy shit!" The look in his eyes as they ran up and down the length of her body made her nipples pebble against the cotton, every raspy breath she took caused delicious friction that sent a jolt of sexual anticipation straight to her groin.

He stood there, half-naked and proud, wearing nothing more than faded jeans that hung low around his slender hips. She wondered idly if he wore anything under them. He was barefoot and topless after a shower, showcasing his impressive abdominal muscles. Her heart ached for him and she found herself mesmerized by the fluid movement of the muscles under his skin, the dragon on his left shoulder looked as though it were dancing, each muscle contracted and relaxed as he seemed to fight for a measure of control. When he eventually turned back to the stove, she took a seat at the breakfast bar facing the kitchen.

"Were you planning on getting dressed today?" his voice was strained as if he had forced the words through gritted teeth. "Don't get me wrong, you look great, especially as I can see

through it, but I can feel your eyes on me and it's -
" he paused as if searching his vocabulary for the
right word," - to be frank it's driving me crazy".

She crossed her arms over her chest to restrict
the level of exposure, but the look in his eyes, the
hunger she'd seen there had stripped away
everything. He didn't turn around as he fired
another question at her. "Are you afraid of me?"

"No. You're my protector, if I can't trust you
who can I trust?" she answered without hesitation.
That seemed to please him.

He turned the stove off as he plated up her
meal. "It's novel to have food in the house. I don't
think I've ever used the kitchen before!" She
looked over her shoulder and into the dining room,
where a very sturdy dining table stood proud. It
was big enough to seat 12 easily, but all her
movement achieved was to draw his attention to
her slender neck and the pulse beating an erratic
rhythm there.

"Looks like you entertain all the time." He
shook his head in response.

"I've never invited another soul into my
home. I try to keep people away."

"Then why did you bring me here?" He'd
been asking himself the same question, he could
have taken her to a hotel, kept an eye on her in her
own apartment even, but something inside him
had screamed at him to bring her back here. The
place he owned, full of his possessions - and now

he'd placed her in that same category. She was *his*.

"Seccombe has a very keen personal interest in you, and this list of yours - at some point we're going to talk about that." He turned to leave her in the kitchen as she finished the remainder of her meal, but the air suddenly started cracking and popping with electricity and that only happened when a powerful vampire was about to announce his presence.

"Hayden, what's the matter?" He didn't respond; instead, his attention zeroed in on the doorway where he knew the visitor would appear.

"Hayden, you're starting to scare me…"
"We're about to have a visitor." A heartbeat later, Jackson phased into the kitchen, much to his relief. "You prick! Why didn't you call me? I was getting ready to rip your throat out."

"How do women keep their hands off you with charm like that?" Jackson's words brought him back to earth with a bump; Amelia had come to stand beside him and she was still wearing nearly nothing, and there was another man in the room getting an eyeful. Jackson extended a hand to her, "Dr Jameson, it's nice to finally meet you, I'm Jackson."

"Likewise," she started to step forward to take his hand, the movement hitched the fabric of the shirt up her thighs minutely but that was enough to push Hayden over the edge. He stepped between them and turned to face her, unaware of what he was going to say until the moment came - but it didn't matter, she beat him to it. She stood tall, pushed her shoulders back and looked him straight in the eye; it reminded him of how she looked after her shower yesterday. He hadn't left the room, even though she expected him to, he thought he could handle it - dared her, even - but when it came down to it and she started to undress, he had to get out of there, he just didn't trust himself with her.

"Look, I have just as much right to know what's going on as you do." He loved how strong she was, but right now he didn't want her brave and bold - he wanted her out of the room and away from Jackson's hungry eyes.

"We work on a need-to-know basis, and right now, you don't need to know." He wouldn't take the words back even if he could, but he would take the look of betrayal she couldn't hide, before she turned and walked away from him.

"Smooth, man. I'd sleep with one eye open if I were you - that's if you're even getting around to sleeping." His tone held a note of petulance.

"Why are you here?"

"Okay, okay. I'll keep it brief because I can see you're anxious having me here with her."

"If you've come to check up on me, there's nothing going on, I'm doing my job and protecting her - nothing more, nothing less. Perhaps you should do yours and find Seccombe."

"There's nothing happening yet, but I see the way you look at her like you're willing to die for her."

"That's my job."

"No. Your job is to make sure no harm comes to her. Times have changed, Hayden, but the law hasn't. You show more control than any other guardian I've ever met, but if you mate with her there will be consequences."

Jackson was right; he was anxious to have him around Amelia and the pull that only subsided when she was near had become an ache in his chest and she was only down the hall.

"And I am doing my job - that's why I'm here, to talk to her about the list."

"You asshole! I thought you weren't involving her in this?!"

"I gave you 24 hours to report back so here I am, whether you like it or not. I will get that information any way I have to."

"That won't be necessary," he said, but hadn't heard Amelia arrive back in the room. Judging by the look on Jackson's face, he hadn't either; she was dressed in dark skinny jeans and a light loose sweater that hung low on one shoulder. Although she was covered more than earlier, he still didn't like so much flesh exposed for anyone else's viewing pleasure.

He turned and headed into the living room, knowing they would both follow him. He eyed his favorite overstuffed chair, but instead went to sit on the couch hoping she'd come and sit by him. Although she sat as far away as possible, she didn't disappoint and flashed him a nervous smile as she curled her legs under her and swept her damp hair out of her face and over one shoulder. The simple move drew his attention again and it took every ounce of self-control to stay put; he'd spent hundreds of thousands of dollars decorating the room to his liking but she was still the most beautiful thing in it.

His eyes dropped to her hands, which were a blur of movement fiddling with the cuff of her sweater. She turned her body towards him and spoke only to him - perhaps he hadn't upset her after all. "It's my blood he wants."

Jackson took a sharp breath and cursed quietly as if his fears were being confirmed.

"Only one percent of the population is AB-. When my paper was published, Elijah contacted me; I guess he knew what it meant and that's what the list is."

"People with AB- blood?" It was more of a statement than a question.

"Yes."

Hayden sank back into the cushions, closed his eyes and pinched the bridge of his nose as reality came crashing down around him. Jackson spoke the words he wasn't able to, "You understand it's not just the taste he craves. Your blood will strengthen him, it will only take one drop to addict him. It's rare for that very reason.

Vampires crave the taste and the power that comes with it."

She shot a glance in his direction. "I've worked with vampires for months; each volunteer that entered my lab has sensed the abnormality in my blood, why didn't you?"

"I haven't fed from a human since I reached maturity, I have an understanding with half a dozen blood banks in the city. It makes sense that Elijah would assign your protection to me, knowing I'm not like my brethren."

"Yeah that's great and all, but it doesn't help us with the problem in hand - how do we get it back from him and stop a massacre?"

He had to work on his anger; he wasn't irritated at her, but at that bastard Seccombe who thought he could have her. Consequences or not, he'd save her and there was really only one way to do that.

If Amelia thought yesterday was a bad day, it was nothing compared to today and it was only going to get worse. "There's something else. My dream last night, well, it was more than a dream. The vampire from the club was there - Travis? It was like he was trying to communicate with me."

Jackson was up and pacing the floor, only sparing her a quick glance to ask what he'd said in this dream.

"He told me to renounce my protection and to go to him. He didn't say where, but he showed me. There's a concrete compound about forty miles from here, surrounded by grassland, fences and guards."

"We must act!" She could see Jackson trying to think of a way to use it to their advantage; Hayden referred to the clan as his brethren and Jackson, in particular, was like a brother, but the look he gave his adoptive sibling was lethal.

"No fucking way. Whatever you're thinking of, the answer is no." One minute, Jackson was wearing a hole in the antique rug and the next Hayden had him pinned against the wall.

"Think about it, Hayden. If she goes to Seccombe we'll have an advantage, a way to get in, and we can get her out before anything happens."

"If you send her in there you're signing her death warrant."

"If her protection is renounced, then it's nothing to do with you any more."

'She' hated being spoken about like she wasn't in the room. The two vampires were going at it and she had to move once or twice to avoid sheetrock debris, as each took a turn slamming the other against the wall.

"How do I do it?" her voice was small amongst the fray but both men heard her and froze.

"What the fuck?! Amelia, y-you can't do that! Are you insane?" Hayden moved quicker than her brain could register, until he was crowding over her, his devastatingly handsome face etched in horror. "Do you want to die?"

"I want to save those people on the list, and I want to stop Seccombe. Jackson's right - this is the only way."

"I'll update Elijah and give you two a moment alone." Jackson left the room, and suddenly Hayden's hands reached up to cup her face; he waited until her eyes met his before he spoke.

"Please don't do this Em. For me, I'm begging you," he pleaded, his eyes giving away the depth of his emotion. All she wanted to do was obey him, tell him she'd do anything he ever asked, if only he'd promise to look at her like that forever.

"Why do you help people?"

"This isn't about me."

"Just tell me!"

"It's my job. More than that - it's my duty."

"And this is mine." Unable to stop herself, she reached for his stubbled jaw; the texture was rough in her palm as she caressed him. He closed his eyes briefly and leant into her touch, and coming up on her toes, she tentatively brushed her mouth against his. He responded immediately with a feral growl, splaying his fingers at her nape and pulling her mouth closer, taking the kiss deeper. One minute he had his hands in her hair and the next he lifted her so she could wrap her legs around his waist. Thank God he still hadn't put a shirt on - she didn't waste a second. He plastered her up against the wall while her hands explored his body. Their kisses became fierce and desperate, both needing a release from the tension and desire that had been building between them.

Something inside her changed in that moment. This new feeling could be dwelled upon later because, for now, she was content to feel his breath come and go with hers. His lips moved along her jaw then down to her neck where her pulse beat out an erratic rhythm. Then, as quickly as it had begun, it was over. The room was silent except for the sound of their labored breathing, he kissed her lips again, slightly swollen from the intensity of his mouth. Once, twice, three times, before he phased.

When Jackson reentered the room, he looked around for Hayden before fixing his speculative gaze on her; he must have known what had just happened. She was leaning against the wall for support - blushing, panting and trembling - he didn't say anything, but instead ushered her out of the room

"We need to meet with Elijah. We're running out of time, so you'll go to Seccombe tonight. We can't guarantee what will happen between leaving our protection and when we storm the compound."

"I know. Shouldn't we wait for Hayden?" She missed him already.

"He'll meet us there, it seems there are some things he also needs to speak with Elijah about."

Chapter Three

It was nightfall when they arrived at headquarters, and after spending an hour with Elijah and Jackson, Amelia was desperate to have a few moments alone with Hayden, but the only time he even acknowledged her was when Elijah asked him to sign the Termination of Protection Agreement. His eyes, full of regret and betrayal, held hers for a moment before he scrawled on the page and left the room.

"Jackson will take you as far as the boundary line, you'll have to continue on foot from there but I anticipate you won't be alone for very long." It was hard to believe that Elijah had lived for over a century and a half for he still looked like a young man with black, shoulder-length hair and kind grey eyes. "This is a very noble and brave move, Dr Jameson, it's a great sacrifice."

It wasn't a sacrifice, not in her eyes, and she hoped that one day Hayden could forgive her for this decision and realize that she did it for him as much as the other people on her stupid list. She slowly slipped on her jacket as Jackson approached holding a small black box.

"This is a GPS tracking device, so we can pinpoint your location in the compound. I think you'll be safe for the first hour - he needs you to decrypt your work before he can kill you. Don't worry, we'll be gatecrashing after thirty minutes."

"That'll be the first thing they search for when they take her," the strained voice came from the back of the room.

"Would you rather she went without it?" Silence. "I thought not. Okay Amelia, we need to get going. Are you ready?" She'd vowed to herself that she'd do anything to keep those people safe.

"Yes." Her voice sounded more assertive than she felt but she'd made her decision.

He looked over her shoulder, and in more of a statement than a question, he asked, "I take it you're coming too?"

Hayden approached her from behind, she could feel the vibration of every footstep as he got closer and closer. Soon a strong hand rested on her shoulder, a show of alliance and loyalty. There was no question Hayden was in this too, until the end.

He didn't just hate this idea, he fucking hated it. He'd spent the last three months protecting this little human, getting lost in stories about her childhood and laughing at the way she messed up the punchline of a joke.

He'd stayed awake all night, watching her sleep, wondering what she was dreaming about -

how those soft sighs would feel against skin as she lay next to him. He'd lost all coherent thoughts this morning when he'd seen her standing there in nothing but his shirt. It took every ounce of self-control not to go to her, back her up to the table, rip the shirt and expose her flesh to him. Yep, somewhere along the line, he'd fallen for her. Fallen hard.

She'd been studying him as they entered the car, but he knew exactly what she was doing because he was doing the same thing.

"Don't look at me like that!"

"Like what?" She'd been acting nonchalantly since their kiss earlier.

"Like you're trying to memorize my face… You have thirty minutes, then I'm coming in to find you. If you die, I'll kill you!"

The sound of her laughter wrapped around him like an embrace and, without thinking about it, he took her hand and placed it in his. Her eyes followed the movement then met his own, "I'll keep that in mind."

"We'll reach the boundary line in about two minutes," he comforted. Jackson was driving, allowing Hayden to sit in the back of the jeep with Amelia. He didn't want to waste a moment of time with her knowing this could be the last time they were together. "When we get back and I've cleaned the mess in the living room, I'm going to buy you a grand piano so you can play to me all day. I'll covert your talent for myself."

He leaned into her, so close his breath fanned across her cheek, and took a moment to inhale her scent - Jasmine and Sweet Violet - committing it to memory.

"Hayden. We're here"

"Okay, just give me a minute." Jackson eyed him for a second, before giving a single nod and killing the engine. Without loosening the grip on her hand, he exited the car, taking Amelia with him and as soon as she closed the door he pinned her up against it.

"We have unfinished business."

"W - What do you mean?" she was breathless and, right now, he didn't give a damn about anything else other the taste of her.

"We started something earlier, something I'm desperate to have again."

"I - I can't - we can't. The law…" he knew what she was trying to say and reveled in the fact he could affect her to the point where she couldn't form a sentence. He reached up and ran his fingers through her hair, reading her reaction - she wanted him too.

"The law no longer applies to us, sweetness. You renounced your protection, I'm no longer your guardian." He brushed his lips against hers, the fire he felt from that brief touch was intense, but not enough; he pressed his lips fully against hers and groaned as she parted them, letting him taste her heat once more. The fire between them grew into an inferno, she met every thrust of his tongue with her own as her hands locked behind his neck, refusing to let him go. God, he liked that thought, and only when they both struggled to breathe did he end the kiss and rest his forehead against hers.

"Please come back to me, Em."

Her neck and pulse drew his attention – and the attention of his lips – as he placed open-mouthed kisses down to her collarbone. When his lips traced her carotid artery, it took an enormous amount of willpower to stop his fangs from descending - now wasn't the time. Her taste was vibrant on his tongue, her scent filling every part of him. A nip over the vein followed by a sweep of his tongue had her tilting her head back, offering. She wants this too. Take her. Mark her and make her yours. Before it's too late.

Leaving a wet trail along the slender column of her neck, he claimed her mouth again, lips parted in invitation as his tongue dueled with hers. But he wanted more - wanted to be wrapped in her heat, while he buried himself deep inside her. The thought would have had him instantly hard, if he wasn't already.

"I want to do this with you forever, and I know that's what you want too. Forever is half an hour away, Em." He kissed her once more - a brief touch of lips, a promise before letting her go.

Once she disappeared into the darkness, he climbed back into the jeep to stop himself from running after her. When he settled himself back into his seat and set his watch for 30 minutes, Jackson shot him a teasing glance. "Pleased to see me?"

He shamelessly reached down to adjust himself, embarrassed. "It's not for you!"

"Wow dude, you've got it bad," Jackson joked, punching his friend's arm in comradeship.

"Tell me about it. I hate this whole fucked-up situation - there must have been another way."

"Your doctor is far too important to the clan, no one would risk her if there was any other way."

He knew there was only truth in his brother's words but he just couldn't shake the images of her, helpless against Seccombe's rogues, desperate to devour her. "Where's the GPS receiver?"

Jackson handed over the small screen that resembled a satellite navigation system. It didn't take a genius to work out that the blue flashing dot moving slowly across the screen was Amelia. She'd just reached the boundary line and was heading towards the compound. Each second was unbearable but the minutes were torturous; he'd looked at his watch fourteen times in the last four minutes.

"Dude, seriously, it's not even been five minutes and already you're driving me crazy!"

"I can't just sit here and do nothing - she's in there unprotected."

"It was her choice."

"Some choice - kill or be killed!"

"You will sit there and do nothing, or I'll pull rank on you, soldier!" Jackson only jested, but the warning was real.

"I'd love to see you try and stop me." The reality was that no one could - the laws were right to forbid mating. He felt so fiercely protective of Amelia - he was pretty sure he'd even hurt Jackson to make sure she was safe - and he could only imagine what it would have been like had they actually mated. He probably would have driven a stake into the guy's heart for even suggesting she go into the compound. Hayden had to distract himself, so thought back to the feel of Amelia's body against his as he'd pinned her to the car, the shock as he'd kissed her, then the moment she'd melted in his arms. He might not have mated with her, but he had claimed her and any other vampire who would cross her would know that; a smile played along the edge of his lips as he thought about all the ways in which he'd claim her body.

"I can't take much more of this," Jackson complained, "I don't know what's worse - you sitting there like a abandoned lovesick puppy, or you sitting there like a horny vampire!"

"You'll understand one day, my friend!" At that moment, the blue flashing dot stopped moving. They looked at each other, neither needed to say anything to know what the other was thinking. Amelia was in the compound.

"Tell me again why we're waiting half an hour, because at this moment in time, I can't think of one God-damned reason…"

"We need to give them time to take her to Seccombe; if we go rushing in there and we don't get him, this whole thing is a waste of time. She won't ever be safe unless we take him and the organisation down." His friend tried to distract him with questions about Amelia, and what happened the night before: "She mentioned seeing Travis at the club, there's only a handful of clubs where super naturals can hang out."

"Just drop it will you? She didn't want anyone to know, and I'll be damned if I'm going to tell you!" Since when had he put his loyalty to Amelia before his brethren? He didn't have time to think about that now, because the blue dot vanished from his screen.

"Fuck!" he snarled. "I knew they'd search her, we have to get her out of there!"

"Wait! We knew this might happen, there's fifteen minutes left. Hold tight."

He tried to clear his head. He knew they'd find the tracking device and Amelia was strong, she'd stood toe to toe with him, time after time. Just fifteen minutes and he'd have her in his arms again.

"Son of a bitch!" Hc clutched his chest, as a sharp pain shot straight through his heart - it's what he imagined being staked would feel like.

"What is it?" There was, however, no chance to respond to his friend's worried words. The pain became unbearable and then everything went black. "Hayden! Hayden!" He opened his eyes but his vision was blurry, he had to blink several times to clear it.
"A-Amelia?"

"What the hell happened? You just blacked out!"

"She's hurt. I felt it - I can still feel it…"

"What? How come?"

"That doesn't matter right now, we have to get her out!"

"You can't go anywhere until you recover."
"If the pain stops, that means she's dead. At the minute I'm glad for the agony - we can use it to find her, call it a built-in GPS!" At that, he threw open the car door and took off across the muddy field closely followed by Jackson, "The closer I get to her, the less pain I'll feel until I find her."

"Or until she's been killed…" Hayden didn't appreciate the reminder, but it did make him run faster; all this time, he thought the pull in his chest was the guardian side of him keeping tabs on her, but in reality it was so much more - her heart called out to his. He scaled the perimeter fence in seconds and made short work of the two guards who got in his way.

"If you go running in there like this, you're forcing his hand and into making into a rash decision." But he couldn't hear, or didn't want to; adrenaline was pumping through his veins - all he cared about was finding Amelia alive and cutting down anyone who got in the way.

They encountered four more soldiers lying in a heap by the solid steel door. Wires and what looked like C4 were being fastened to the door as they approached, and Jackson knocked him to the ground as the explosives detonated. If Seccombe didn't know he had company before, he definitely did now. Fifteen warriors made their way through the gaping hole one by one, without hesitation. Hayden's faith in Elijah had been restored; Amelia clearly was a valuable commodity and he must have wanted her back at headquarters just as much as Hayden himself did.

The guards came at them thick and fast, fifty-plus, all armed with guns loaded with wooden bullets. A few grazed his arms as he took out another three rogues.
"Are you going to leave any for the rest of us?! Concentrate on locating your woman - that's how we'll find Seccombe!"

The ache in his chest subsided considerably as he turned onto the second corridor, and the sound of heavy footsteps at his heels told him Jackson and his team had his back. He paused outside a locked door, but Jackson grabbed his arm before he could take another step.

"I'm picking up six entities, but all of them are human. Seccombe isn't here - he's been gone for hours and there's not enough of an energy trail to follow. We've lost him."

With one kick, the wooden door flew off its hinges and crashed against the far wall in the room. Female screams filled the air as he and Jackson entered the room. In the corner - huddled together and scared to within an inch of their lives - one of the four looked as young as seventeen, but he wasn't interested in them. Tied to the bed was his reason for living - elegant hands and feet bound to the bed frame, eyes closed, but he could see the rise and fall of her chest. The pain disappeared. She was alive.

"Amelia!" he cried, taking two steps towards her, before realizing there was someone there with her. The sixth woman - she was shielding Amelia with her body.

"Get them out of here! I'm taking Amelia home with me!"

"You can't phase with her, you know what it'll do to you…"

"I don't have a choice, I need her with me. Please brother, if I never ask you for anything again - please grant me this!" he begged.

Jackson approached the women in the corner with caution and soothing tones. "Take them back to headquarters, Elijah will want to speak with them," then he turned his attention back to the woman with Amelia. She must have been in her late twenties, with dirty blonde hair and a confused expression on her face.

"Are you H-Hayden?" He approached the bed and lifted Amelia's hand to his lips.

"I am, and you are?" he asked, as the last of the four women left the room, leaving himself, Jackson and the two women on the bed alone.

"I'm Mya. She spoke about you - called out for you when they chained her up." He tested her restraints but they didn't give easily

"Mya, look at me, what happened here?"

"The blonde one. I don't know his name, but he bought her here, shouting about a list. He threatened to kill us. And her, if she didn't help them." He searched the room as she explained.

"Then what?" his patience grew shorter with every second she was bound.

"He tied her up and extracted a vial of her blood. None of us could stop him but she didn't give up - she bit him then he hit her and she hasn't woken up since."

"Take her back with the others," Hayden decreed, as Jackson started to lead her out of the room, "Thank you, Mya." He turned to Jackson, "I'll follow!"

The compound was empty now his team had left, so gingerly he moved closer to her. "Amelia, Amelia honey? Can you hear me?"

Her head was full of fog, and throbbing at the temples, but there was something - someone who needed her. She tried to open her eyelids but thcy felt too heavy.

"That's it baby, open your eyes for me!" It was Hayden - he was here! She tried again, this time with more success.

"It - it was a trap. S - Seccombe isn't here." Was that her voice?

"I know baby, I need to get you home. That means I have to break these chains, it might hurt a little."

"Just do it!" she affirmed. Her muscles were strained by the tight chains, she could see his biceps bulge through his shirt as he broke through her restraints. Two things seemed to happen simultaneously: she heard her bonds break and at the same time the air changed. It now felt like it had this morning, before Jackson had appeared. From what Hayden had said, the vampire was long gone, along with the other hostages. She looked up at Hayden as he helped her to sit upright. He looked almost glad.

"It's Travis, I was hoping he'd come back but I'd have liked to get you out of here first. Stay put." Like she could move even if she'd wanted to, she thought, for her limbs were screaming out in protest to every minute movement.

"Well well. What do we have here? You appear to have taken my girls, but left me with the best one!" He was standing in the doorway blocking the exit, not that Hayden would have saved himself. He'd die here if he had to, and that thought alone scared her more than being killed by Travis.

"Hayden, please go! You don't have to protect me any more."

Travis patronized, "She's a smart little thing, isn't she? You should listen to her, I don't much like an audience but I'm willing to make an exception for you, guardian!" Hayden with his dark features, flew at the blonde vampire, and the force of the two men colliding was enough to make the building shake. They were like thunder and lightning, never striking in the same place twice. The pair separated briefly, both spitting blood. All the while, her eyes never left Hayden; his clothes were ripped, had that happened earlier when he'd taken on the guards or was Travis too strong? No, she wouldn't believe that, but then he had taken a vial of her blood earlier. There wasn't much she could do - she couldn't fight, even if she could move without flinching.

"Hayden," she extended a bloody arm where the chains had bitten into her flesh.

"You need it more than I do baby!" he charged Travis again. This time, though, he seemed to be in a dozen places at once; Hayden had his nemesis completely disorientated before unsheathing a blade from his belt and sinking it into the blonde vampire's chest. A few seconds later, there was just the two of them.

"Now we can leave!" She tried to stand, but her feet gave way beneath her. Hayden managed to hook an arm around her waist before she fell on her behind. "You can't carry me, you're hurt."

"I'm not going to carry you!" He held her tighter - as if that were possible - and claimed her mouth. One minute, they were in a blood-soaked cell inside Seccombe's concrete compound; the next, they were back at Hayden's estate.

"I thought phasing someone with you drained your energy?"
"What can I say?! It seems you're my own personal reserve tank!" He kissed her again before she could respond.

He lay atop her on his bed, brushing her hair out of her face marveling at how perfectly his body fit hers.

"When I walked into that room and you were lying there, tied up and unconscious, I thought I'd lost you. I've never felt pain like that." And that was really saying something, after the pain that had caused him to blackout. "I can't ever lose you Em."

"Then don't!" she agreed. Every touch of her lips sent a shock to his long dormant heart. He'd once thought himself incapable of love, but looking at his little human that now seemed absurd. He was the only one capable of loving her - loving her like she needed and loving her like she wanted. He nipped at her skin and longed to let his fangs penetrate her flesh and devour her. Frantic hands ripped and tore at cloth until they were both naked. He then positioned himself on top of her again, holding onto the last shreds of his self-control.

"You're mine!" He forced himself to take it slowly as he claimed her, but her nails in his back undid him; instead, he kissed her with a passion that should have set the room on fire.

"Please Hayden, oh God please!" He loved it when she used his name. Coming from her lips it sounded sweeter than any music he'd ever known.

"Fuck!" he snarled, voice strained. He was on the edge, and as he fell into oblivion, he sank his teeth into her flesh. His body pulsed inside her as the blood in turn pulsed at her neck, filling his mouth, and joining them in every way. The second his fangs penetrated her vain, an exploding supernova took over his body, sending sparks everywhere and consuming his every thought until there was only the two of them.

He felt nothing but pure bliss, lying on top of this gorgeous woman. It was the single most incredible thing he'd ever experienced, and when she'd pleaded for his bite and begged him to claim her, there was no way he could deny it - his body craved the connection too. He felt her blood flowing through his veins, caressing his heart and filling him with new strength. He felt every drop coursing through his system, throbbing as if it was composed of pure power. When he rolled onto his back, he bought her with him to lie on his chest as he put his lips to her hair. "I can feel the strength of your blood in my veins. It's amazing!"

His hands moved slowly down her cheeks until they rested on her neck, where he'd marked her moments earlier.

"Your scent is intoxicating to me - not just your blood but everything about you." He paused for a minute, inhaling deeply. "This mark means you're mine to protect, mine to cherish mine and mine to love." He let the word hang there for a few seconds before adding, "You're mine, Amelia, and I'll cut down anyone who thinks they can take you from me."

"Yes, I'm getting that impression!" she joked.

She'd longed for this man like the live music at Indigo; he awakened her soul and filled her with a sense of belonging. She'd been to hell and back to find the place she belonged in the world - in Hayden's arms. She belonged to this man, to her vampire.

67